Solomon
Crocodile

For Colin x

First published 2011 by Macmillan Children's Books
This edition published 2012 by Macmillan Children's Books
a division of Macmillan Publishers Limited
20 New Wharf Road, London N1 9RR
Basingstoke and Oxford
Associated companies throughout the world
www.panmacmillan.com

ISBN: 978-1-4472-2743-4

Text and illustrations copyright © Catherine Rayner 2011
Moral rights asserted.

1 3 5 7 9 8 6 4 2

A CIP catalogue record for this book is available
from the British Library.

Printed in Belgium

Catherine Rayner

Solomon Crocodile

Macmillan Children's Books

All is peaceful on the banks of the
river. Everyone is relaxing in
the morning sun, until...

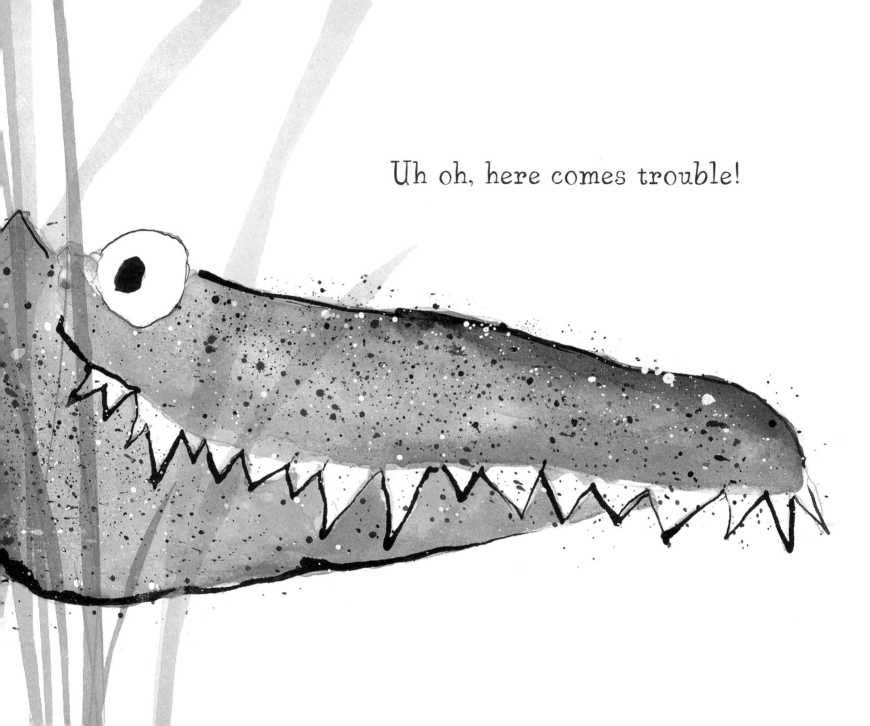

Uh oh, here comes trouble!

Solomon splats and slops
through the mud to make
the frogs jump.

But the frogs croak,
"Go away Solomon, you're
nothing but a pest."

So Solomon shakes
the bulrushes and
bugs the dragonflies.

But the dragonflies sing, "Go away Solomon, you're nothing but a nuisance."

Solomon decides to stalk the storks.
They get in such a flap!

"Go away Solomon," the
storks squawk, "you're
nothing but a pain."

Out of the corner of his eye,
Solomon spies the biggest
hippo in the river.

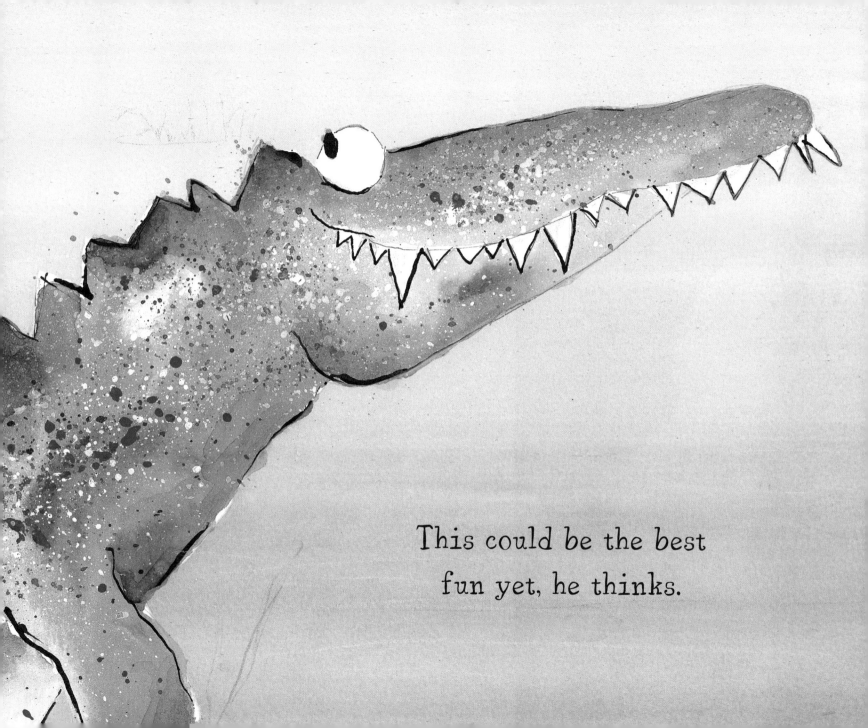

This could be the best
fun yet, he thinks.

Solomon charges!

But...

"SOLOMON," roars the biggest hippo, "GO AWAY! YOU'RE NOTHING BUT TROUBLE!"

Poor Solomon.
No one wants to play.

But then Solomon hears a noise.

Somebody is making the frogs jump.

Somebody is bugging the dragonflies.

And **somebody** has the storks in a flap...

but it is NOT Solomon.

Somebody is getting nearer...

and **nearer**...

Uh oh, here comes . . .

DOUBLE
TROUBLE!